Romeo & Juliet

William Shakespeare

Adapted by
Anna Claybourne

Illustrated by Jana Costa

Reading consultant: Alison Kelly
Roehampton University

Characters in the story

Old Montague,
head of the
Montague family

Count Paris,
a nobleman

Prince Escalus,
ruler of
Verona

Benvolio,
Romeo's cousin

Romeo
Montague

Mercutio,
Romeo's friend

Contents

Chapter 1

Capulets and Montagues

It was a warm summer's afternoon in the pretty town of Verona. People were busy shopping and chatting in the sunshine when suddenly...

Two gangs of young men tore across the market square, fighting, kicking and rolling in the dust. The townspeople ran for cover.

The gangs belonged to two of Verona's richest families – the Capulets and the Montagues. The families were sworn enemies, and they were always fighting.

In minutes, Verona's ruler Prince Escalus arrived with his soldiers to break up the fight. The prince was furious.

"I've had enough of this feud!" he raged. "It's got to stop. From now on, anyone caught fighting will be put to death!"

Old Montague, the head of the Montague family, hurried into the market square, searching for his son Romeo. But he only found Benvolio, Romeo's cousin.

Where's Romeo? Is he safe?

"Don't worry, uncle," said Benvolio. "Romeo wasn't fighting. He's too sensible."

8

Soon after that, Romeo himself
wandered by. Benvolio was telling
him what had happened, when
someone spoke behind them.

Have you heard?
Old Capulet's holding a
masked ball tonight.

"Did you hear that, Romeo?" whispered Benvolio. "A party at the Capulets' house. Let's go! If we wear disguises, no one will guess who we are."

That's a brilliant idea!

Excitedly, the two young Montagues went to find their friend Mercutio, to invite him along.

Chapter 2

Falling in love

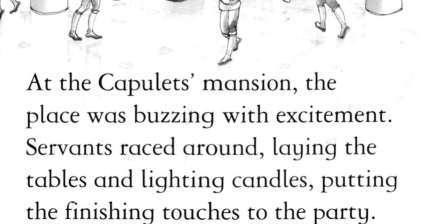

At the Capulets' mansion, the place was buzzing with excitement. Servants raced around, laying the tables and lighting candles, putting the finishing touches to the party.

Upstairs, Juliet Capulet's nurse was helping her dress, when Juliet's mother came in.

"Now Juliet," she said. "A man named Count Paris is coming tonight. I hope you like him. Your father and I want you to marry him."

But I'm only thirteen!

"Oh Juliet, sweetheart," squealed her nurse. "You're to be married! How exciting!"

Juliet was horrified. She wasn't ready to get married. And what if she *didn't* like Count Paris?

But there was no time to argue. The party was about to start. Straightening her dress, Juliet went down the grand marble staircase to the banqueting hall.

13

A little later, three surprise guests arrived. Benvolio and Mercutio wanted to dance, but Romeo stood still.

He had spotted a beautiful girl in a pink and cream dress and he couldn't take his eyes off her.

Who is that girl? She's lovely.

Juliet's cousin Tybalt recognized the three friends and went straight to Old Capulet. "Uncle, there are Montagues here!" he declared. "Let's kick them out."

"No, Tybalt," said his uncle. "Remember the prince's warning."

We don't want to start a fight.

Romeo saw the girl leave the hall and followed. Shyly, he went up to her. "I don't know who you are," he said, "but I've fallen in love with you. You're beautiful!" And he kissed her.

Juliet had left the hall to escape from Count Paris. She didn't like Paris at all. But when Romeo kissed her, she felt her heart fluttering. She fell in love with him at once.

"Who are you?" Juliet murmured.

"He's Romeo Montague!" snapped Juliet's nurse, who had come to look for her. "And Old Capulet would have a fit if he saw his daughter with a Montague. Come on," she urged, taking Juliet away. "Count Paris wants to dance with you."

You're Juliet *Capulet?*

Romeo groaned. "She's a Capulet? What am I going to do?"

When the party ended, Romeo sneaked outside and hid in the Capulets' garden.

As the moon rose, he saw Juliet step onto a balcony. "Oh, Romeo!" she sighed. "It's you I love. If only you weren't a Montague!"

"Juliet," Romeo called to her. "I'm here in the garden. And I love you."

"You do?" said Juliet.

"With all my heart," Romeo replied. "I'd marry you, if I could."

"But my parents are going to make me marry Count Paris," Juliet wailed.

She frowned. "Our only hope is to get married in secret," she said at last.

"Then we will," said Romeo.

"I'll ask my nurse to help us," Juliet decided. "Send me a message tomorrow."

"I will," Romeo promised, "but now I'd better go. Goodbye Juliet!"

Chapter 3

A secret wedding

The next morning, Romeo went to
visit Friar Laurence. The friar was
a wise monk who made medicines
and helped people with problems.

"What can I do for you, Romeo?" Friar Laurence asked.

"I'm in love with Juliet Capulet," Romeo explained. "I know our parents won't like it, but we really want to get married."

"Then I'll help you," the friar said, kindly. "When your parents find out you're married, it might help stop the fighting. If you both come to my house this afternoon, I'll marry you in secret."

Romeo was delighted. He ran to the market square to find Juliet's nurse and give her the message.

The nurse rushed off to tell Juliet what Romeo had said. She hated to see her beloved Juliet unhappy.

Friar Laurence will marry you this afternoon!

Juliet couldn't stop smiling. "I'll tell my parents I'm going to see the friar about my wedding to Count Paris," she decided.

As the clock struck two, Juliet
arrived at Friar Laurence's house.
Romeo was waiting for her and the
friar performed the secret wedding
at once.

You are now
husband and wife!

Romeo and Juliet were married. But Juliet's parents were expecting her back and she had to go straight home.

So Romeo went to look for Benvolio and Mercutio.

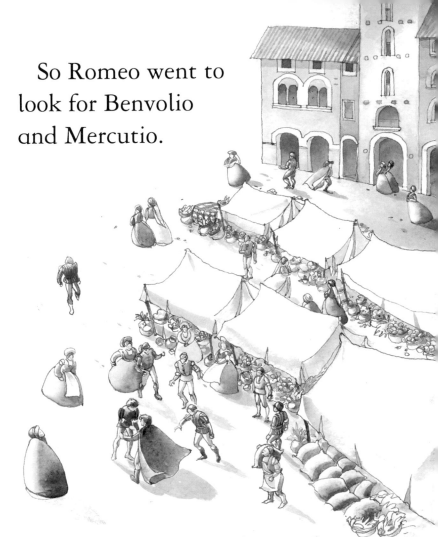

He found them in the market square, arguing with Tybalt Capulet. "What's the problem?" Romeo asked.

27

"You Montagues are the problem," snarled Tybalt, turning to Romeo. "You sneaked into our party and I'm going to make you pay. I challenge you to a duel!"

"I refuse," Romeo replied. "You know the prince said no fighting."

"You're afraid to fight!" Tybalt taunted him.

Coward!

"Don't speak to my friend like that!" said Mercutio.

"Oh, so you want to fight instead, do you?" Tybalt shouted, drawing his sword. Mercutio drew his too, and they started fighting.

"Stop it!" yelled Benvolio. He and Romeo frantically tried to pull the pair apart. They were too late. Tybalt stabbed Mercutio, who slumped to the ground – dead.

Romeo was so upset, he grabbed Mercutio's sword. Without thinking, he ran at Tybalt and stabbed him too.

Benvolio stared in horror as Tybalt sank to the ground. "Romeo, what have you done?" he gasped. "Quick, go before the prince comes!"

Romeo dropped the sword and ran for his life.

Chapter 4

Escape to Mantua

When Prince Escalus arrived,
Benvolio told him about the fight.
The prince was angry but he could
see Tybalt was mostly to blame.
"Romeo shall not die," he said.
"I'll banish him instead."

31

Being banished meant Romeo would have to leave Verona and never come back. It was better than being put to death – but not much.

Oh no! Poor Juliet!

Gossip spread fast in Verona and the nurse soon heard what had happened. With tears in her eyes, she went to tell Juliet.

Juliet was heartbroken. "Cousin Tybalt is dead," she sobbed, "and I'll never see my Romeo again!"

"Don't cry," begged the nurse. "I'll bring Romeo to see you before he leaves. He's hiding at the friar's house."

"Yes, please find him," Juliet said, wiping her eyes. "Ask him to come and say goodbye."

The nurse went straight to the friar's house. Romeo looked as if he'd been crying too.

"Romeo, you should be grateful," said Friar Laurence. "The prince has spared your life."

"But I'm banished," Romeo said. "And I want to be with Juliet."

I love her!

"Go and see her tonight," said the friar, "but make sure you leave Verona by dawn. Head for the city of Mantua. After a while, I'll talk to the prince. I'll ask him to forgive you and let you come home."

The nurse smiled at Romeo. "And I'll tell Juliet you're on your way."

That night, Romeo went
again to the Capulets' garden
and climbed up the ivy to
Juliet's balcony.

Juliet!

Romeo!

But before dawn,
Romeo had to leave.
"It's not time yet,"
Juliet pleaded.
Romeo sighed.
Giving his new wife
one last kiss, he
climbed down the
balcony, sped from
the garden and set
off for Mantua.

36

All that morning, Juliet cried and cried. Her nurse tried to comfort her, but she couldn't stop. Suddenly, her mother and father swept in.

"Poor Juliet," said her mother, going over to her. "You're still upset about Tybalt. But this will cheer you up. You're to marry Count Paris. The wedding's on Thursday!"

37

"Thursday?" Juliet gasped. It was so soon. "And I don't want to marry Count Paris. Please don't make me." Her father scowled.

"I won't marry him," Juliet shouted. "No, no, no!"

"What do you mean, no?" said her father angrily. "You'll marry Count Paris on Thursday and that's that!" And her parents left.

"But I'm already married," wept Juliet. "What am I going to do?"

"Well, you can't tell your parents about Romeo," said her nurse.

I think you'll have to marry Count Paris.

The nurse bustled away and Juliet realized only one person could help her. "I must go and see Friar Laurence," she thought.

Chapter 5

The magic potion

Friar Laurence
was planting herbs
in his garden when Juliet arrived.

"Oh friar, please help me," she
begged. "My father says I have to
marry Count Paris on Thursday!"

"But you can't," said the friar.

"You have to help." Juliet was desperate. "I'd rather die than marry Paris. Is there anything you can do?"

The friar thought for a while. "Well," he said finally, "there is one thing that might work."

What is it?

"I'll give you a magic herbal potion," the friar said. "When you drink it, you'll go into a coma. Your body will be cold and it will look as if you're dead. But really, you'll just be in a very deep sleep, which will last for two days."

How will that help?

"Drink the potion tonight. In the morning, your parents will find you and think you're dead. They'll put your body in the Capulet family tomb while they arrange your funeral."

"Then what?" asked Juliet.

"I'll send a messenger to Mantua to tell Romeo the plan," the friar went on. "Two nights from now, you'll wake up. Romeo can come to Verona to rescue you – and you can run away together!"

"I'll do it," said Juliet, bravely.
She held the bottle in a trembling
hand. "Thank you, Friar Laurence."
Clutching the potion tightly, she
turned and ran home.

Back at the Capulet mansion,
Juliet went to talk to her parents.

"I'm sorry I was rude to you," she
said sweetly. "I was upset about
Tybalt. Of course I'll marry Count
Paris on Thursday."

"Good girl," said her mother.

That night, Juliet sat on her bed. Carefully, she uncorked the bottle Friar Laurence had given her and drank every last drop of the bitter potion.

A few moments later, she fell into a deep, deep sleep.

Chapter 6

Romeo returns

It was
just as the friar
had promised. The next morning,
Juliet's nurse found her cold body
lying on the bed and screamed.
"She's dead! Juliet's dead!"

"There'll be no wedding for my
daughter," said Old Capulet, trying
to hold back his tears. "Instead, we
must prepare for a funeral. Carry
her body to the family tomb."

Meanwhile, Friar Laurence wrote a letter to Romeo, explaining everything. He sealed up the letter and gave it to his friend, Friar John, to deliver.

But the news spread fast. Soon, people for miles around had heard about Juliet's death. In Mantua, a servant told Romeo that Capulet's daughter had died.

No! Oh Juliet, my Juliet!

"I'll go back to Verona and find Juliet in the tomb," Romeo sobbed. "Then I'll lie beside her and drink poison, so I die too. That way, we can be together."

Romeo went to find an apothecary. "I need the strongest poison you have," he said.

"You can't buy poison in Mantua. It's against the law," the man told him. But Romeo saw he was poor and offered him forty gold coins. The apothecary quickly handed over a tiny bottle.

One sip of this could kill 20 men. Be careful.

Romeo put the poison in his bag
and headed for Verona
as fast as his horse
could carry him.

By the time Friar John arrived in
Mantua, Romeo had already left.
So the friar set off back to Verona,
without delivering the letter.

Late that night, Romeo arrived in Verona. He crept to the Capulets' house and found the entrance to the tomb. But someone else was already there.

Count Paris!

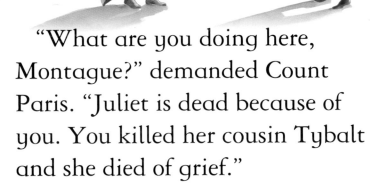

"What are you doing here, Montague?" demanded Count Paris. "Juliet is dead because of you. You killed her cousin Tybalt and she died of grief."

"That's not true!" Romeo cried. "I loved her more than you did."

"You're trespassing," snapped the Count, drawing his dagger. "Get out." He lunged at Romeo.

Romeo drew his dagger too and fought back. Count Paris gasped and fell to his knees, dying.

Oh! I am slain!

Romeo stepped over the body and went to find Juliet. She was lying inside, as cold as the stone beneath her. Romeo took her hand and wept as he kissed her cheek.

She still looks so beautiful – almost as if she's not dead at all.

Back at Friar Laurence's house, Friar John had returned. "I went to Mantua, but I couldn't deliver the message," he announced. "Romeo wasn't there."

Friar Laurence felt sick. "But Juliet will wake up alone in the tomb," he said. "I must rescue her!" And he rushed from his house, heading for the Capulet tomb.

In the tomb, Romeo took out his bottle of poison. He drank it all, lay down beside Juliet and kissed her one last time.

Thus with a kiss, I die.

The poison worked fast. In a few moments, Romeo lay still.

Not long after that, Juliet awoke. She rubbed her eyes and sat up. "Where am I?" she wondered. Then she remembered the magic potion and Friar Laurence's plan.

"Romeo?" she called. "Oh no!" she cried, as she saw his still body. She noticed the poison bottle in his hand and shook his shoulders. He didn't stir.

Juliet realized what he'd done. "Oh Romeo," she sobbed. "I can't live without you. I'll kiss your lips and poison myself too."

Just then she heard a noise. Someone was coming.

Juliet grabbed Romeo's dagger. Before anyone could arrive to stop her, she plunged it into her heart and collapsed on top of Romeo.

Friar Laurence burst into the
tomb, followed by soldiers and
servants. They were too late.
Romeo and Juliet were dead.

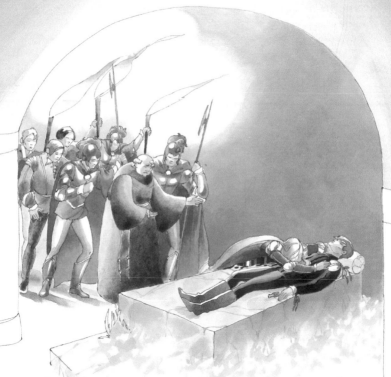

The friar summoned the Capulets,
the Montagues and Prince Escalus
and told them the whole sad story.

The prince turned to the two families. "See what your hatred has done," he said. "Romeo and Juliet have paid the price for your feud."

Old Capulet and Old Montague agreed to bury Romeo and Juliet side by side. Wiping away their tears, they promised that their families would never fight again.

For never was a story of more woe,
Than this of Juliet, and her Romeo.

William Shakespeare
1564 - 1616

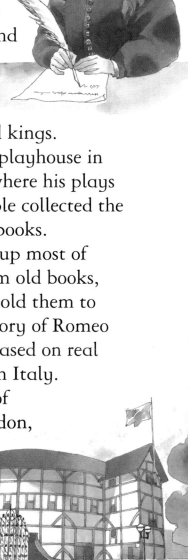

William Shakespeare was a writer who lived in England around 400 years ago. He wrote lots of plays, telling tales of love, marriage, murder, ghosts, witches and kings.

Shakespeare worked at a playhouse in London, called the Globe, where his plays were performed. Later, people collected the plays and made them into books.

Shakespeare didn't make up most of his stories. He got them from old books, folktales or real life, and retold them to make exciting plays. The story of Romeo and Juliet may have been based on real people who lived long ago in Italy.

Today, there is a replica of Shakespeare's Globe in London, where you can see his plays performed.

Series editor: Lesley Sims
Cover design: Russell Punter
Digital manipulation: Mike Olley

Internet links

For links to websites where you can find out more
about Shakespeare, go to the Usborne Quicklinks
Website at **www.usborne-quicklinks.com** and type
the keywords **YR Shakespeare**. Please note that
Usborne Publishing cannot be responsible for the
content of any website other than its own.

First published in 2006 by Usborne Publishing Ltd.,
Usborne House, 83-85 Saffron Hill, London EC1N 8RT, England.
www.usborne.com
Copyright © 2006 Usborne Publishing Ltd.